CW00854369

For Olivia and George

Copyright © 2017, by Gemma Lubbock
The Day the Jellyfish Came Raining Down
Published 2017, by Gemma Lubbock
Bonchester Bridge Hawick TD9 9RZ
SCOTLAND
http://www.gemmalubbock.com
gemmalubbock@gmail.com
An Amazon Publication
Paperback ISBN: **9781521847343**
ALL RIGHTS RESERVED No part of this publication may be
reproduced, stored in a retrieval system, or transmitted in any form
or by any means, electronic, mechanical, photocopying, recording,
scanning, or otherwise, except as permitted under Section 107 or 108
of the 1976 International Copyright Act, without the prior written
permission except in brief quotations embodied in critical articles and
reviews. This novel is entirely a work of fiction. Any resemblance to
actual persons, living or dead, is entirely coincidental.

The Day the Jellyfish Came Raining Down

By Gemma Lubbock

Besha Bonnie Inglenook was a quiet Scottish Town
That is of course until the day the jellyfish came raining down
At first nobody noticed there was anything strange
After all here in Scotland it always rains

Up went umbrellas and on with welly boots
To protect the people from the unusual big gloops,
As the thunder in the air began to roar and rumble
Down from the dark clouds the jellyfish tumbled

Ooh Ya, crivens, heavens to jings
The people are covered in jellyfish stings!

Jellyfish landed where the animals lingered
Their tentacles laced with the most awful of
stingers
More nip than a nettle, more worse as a wasp
More murderous than the maddening midge's
curse
Even the wild Haggis were in need of a nurse

"Ooh Ya, crivens, heavens to jings"
The town began to shout from all the jellyfish
stings

A hot and steamy bowl of porridge
Sat cooling outside a cosy cottage
Through the door came Mrs Myrtle
To stir the porridge with her spurtle
A wheen of jellyfish came hurtling down
And she couped her porridge on the ground

"Ooh Ya, crivens, heavens to jings
Jellyfish for breakfast really does sting!"

Mrs Sprockett from the village shop
Tried to sweep them with a mop
But the jellyfish were everywhere
One got tangled in her hair

Her husband arrived with his trusty sheep
shears
Trimmed away all the jellyfish spears
And left poor Mrs Sprogett
With really cold ears

"Ooh Ya, crivens, heavens to jings,
I really am seek o' these jellyfish things!"

Jock Armstrong appeared in his bonnet and kilt
Stepping about the jellyfish on his pair of stilts
He was quite a dashing picture to behold
His feats of bravery broke the mould
Until all of a sudden he felt something foreign
Glooping and slimy and stuck in his sporran

"Ooh Ya, crivens, heavens to jings
A surprise in your sporran really does sting!"

Taffy the terrier took himself out for a jaunt
Bogling about all his usual haunts
Snuffling the bushes he suddenly rose
With a muckle jellyfish stuck to his nose

Ooh Ya! Poor Taffy, heavens to jings!
It's a trip to the vet for that jellyfish sting!

Onto the scene the firemen arrived
Suited and booted and prepped to survive
They switched on their hoses and swooshed
down the street
But those dastardly jellyfish just could not be
beat

They swam up the torrent and blocked up the
hose
And even found their way to the firemen's
clothes

Ooh Ya, crivens, heavens to jings
The firemen were no match for those jellyfish
stings

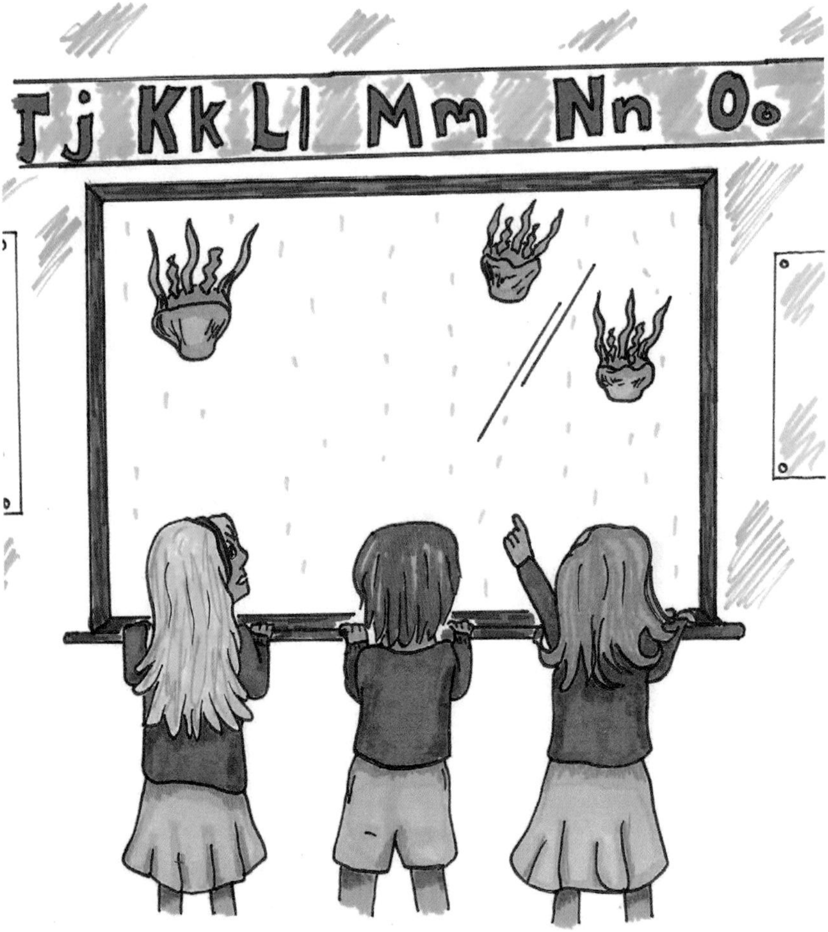
Jj Kk Ll Mm Nn Oo

The children in the classroom could not believe their eyes
"Sit down silly children" the teacher cried
"But it's raining jellyfish" the children replied
"Sit down silly children don't tell such lies!"

The teacher stood in a temper and walked outside
And to all the children's sudden surprise
The horrid teacher met her wicked demise
As a hundred jellyfish fell from the skies

"Ooh Ya, crivens, heavens to jings,
The teacher didn't survive all those jellyfish stings!"

Beatrice MacAlpin drove into town
A reporter sent to film the news going down
Her land rover skidded and crashed to a stop
Through the jellyfish, right into Mrs Sprogett's shop!

The door flew open and out with a plop
Landed Beatrice on her bottom, in for a shock

"Ooh Ya, crivens, heavens to jings
It really does hurt when a jellyfish stings!"

Out came wee Fergus MacDuff from Juniper
Glen
With his big bass drum to rally his men
Riding proud upon his mounted steed
With hooves so fluffy he paid no heed
To the jellyfish lying beneath his feet

The Fifes and Drums gathered at the merket
cross
Drawing their instruments like swords on the
moss
The musicians struck up their mighty chorus
A rousing rendition of the braw Teribus

The jellyfish twitched as if a spell had been cast
Coming to life with each note stronger than the last
They lifted their tentacles and danced to the beat
They danced and marched to the bottom of the street

Fergus led the marching band along the cobbled streets
The dancing jaunty jellies just knew that they'd been beat
They spun and they spiralled right across the shingly shore
Into the wavy water and they were seen no more

The townsfolk realised there was a big mighty feast
They gathered the jellyfish lying about their feet
And before the invaders started to stink
They turned them all into cullen skink!

Besha Bonnie Inglenook was a quiet little town
But they will never quite forget
The day the jellyfish came raining down

The End

How Many Jellyfish Can You Count In The Story?

Glossary:

Bogling	- looking about, exploring
Bonnet	- tartan hat
Couped	- knocked over
Crivens	- an exclamation of surprise
Cullen Skink	- a traditional Scottish fishy dish
Dastardly	- wicked and cruel
Gloops	- big drops
Hurtling	- speeding, fast
Jaunty	- lively and cheerful
Jings!	- this is terrible!
Merket	- market
Moss	- bog, soft wet ground
Muckle	- very big
Seek	- sick
Shingly	- stony, pebbles
Sporran	- a traditional male purse
Spurtle	- wooden kitchen tool for stirring
Swooshed	- moved quickly
Teribus	- traditional song from Hawick
Wheen	- a great number of something

Thank you for reading *The Day the Jellyfish Came Raining Down,* I hope you enjoyed it.

If you bought the book through Amazon, I would be grateful if you could take the time to write a small review on the Amazon sales page.

You might also be interested in reading my other books, please visit www.gemmalubbock.com for more information.